This Walker book bel

_____

_____

_____

For
Catherine and Sarah

First published 1990 by Walker Books Ltd
87 Vauxhall Walk, London SE11 5HJ

This edition published 2010 for Index Books Ltd

2 4 6 8 10 9 7 5 3 1

© 1990 Colin West

The right of Colin West to be identified as author/illustrator of this work has been asserted by him
in accordance with the Copyright, Designs and Patents Act 1988

This book has been typeset in Optima

Printed in China

British Library Cataloguing in Publication Data:
a catalogue record for this book is available from the British Library

ISBN 978-1-4063-2105-0

www.walker.co.uk

"Go tell it to the toucan!"

Colin West

WALKER BOOKS
AND SUBSIDIARIES
LONDON · BOSTON · SYDNEY · AUCKLAND

Hey, today it is my birthday!
thought the elephant one morning.
I'll go tell it to the toucan,
so then he'll tell everybody
all about my birthday party,
and we'll have a jamboree!

So Old Jumbo looked around him
but he couldn't find the toucan,
so instead he told the tiger:
"Hey, today it is my birthday!
Please go tell it to the toucan,
so then he'll tell everybody
all about my birthday party,
and we'll have a jamboree!"

So the tiger looked around him but he couldn't find the toucan, so instead he told the warthog, and the warthog told the hippo:

"Hey, today is Jumbo's birthday!
Please go tell it to the toucan,
so then he'll tell everybody
all about the birthday party,
and we'll have a jamboree!"

So the hippo looked around him
but he couldn't find the toucan,
so instead he told the lion,
and the lion told the bullfrog,
and the bullfrog told the zebra:

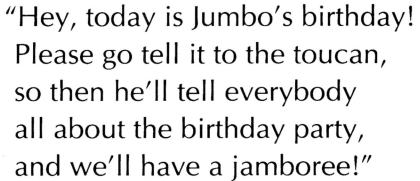

"Hey, today is Jumbo's birthday!
Please go tell it to the toucan,
so then he'll tell everybody
all about the birthday party,
and we'll have a jamboree!"

So the zebra looked around him
but he couldn't find the toucan,
so instead he told the rabbit,
and the rabbit told the rhino,
and the rhino told the lizard,
and the lizard told the panda:

"Hey, today is Jumbo's birthday!
Please go tell it to the toucan,
so then he'll tell everybody
all about the birthday party,
and we'll have a jamboree!"

So the panda looked around him
but he couldn't find the toucan,
so instead he told the ostrich,
and the ostrich told the tortoise,
and the tortoise told the cricket,
and the cricket told the leopard,
and the leopard told the monkey:

"Hey, today is Jumbo's birthday!
Please go tell it to the toucan,
so then he'll tell everybody
all about the birthday party,
and we'll have a jamboree!"

So the monkey looked around him
and upon the highest treetop
at long last he found the toucan!
So the monkey told the toucan
what Old Jumbo told the tiger
what the tiger told the warthog
what the warthog told the hippo
what the hippo told the lion
what the lion told the bullfrog
what the bullfrog told the zebra
what the zebra told the rabbit
what the rabbit told the rhino
what the rhino told the lizard
what the lizard told the panda
what the panda told the ostrich
what the ostrich told the tortoise
what the tortoise told the cricket
what the cricket told the leopard
what the leopard had just told him:

"Hey, today is Jumbo's birthday!
So please go tell everybody
all about the birthday party,
and we'll have a jamboree!"

So the toucan looked around him...

and he looked behind the bushes...

and he looked among the flowers...

and he looked down by the river...

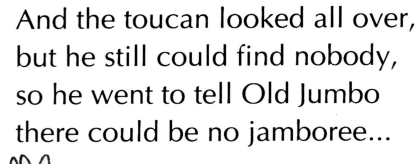

And the toucan looked all over,
but he still could find nobody,
so he went to tell Old Jumbo
there could be no jamboree...

But when the toucan found him,
"Hey, hello there!" cried Old Jumbo.
"Thanks for telling everybody
all about my birthday party...

"You're a really clever toucan.
Come and join the...

Colin West says he chose a toucan as the messenger in
"Go Tell It to the Toucan!" because "with their fabulous bills,
they are such wonderful birds to draw."
He goes on to say, "It was really good fun thinking up the
repetitive lines for the story. But to make them scan,
every animal had to have two syllables in its name –
so the cricket had to be a cricket, and not a grasshopper!"